DEMI'S
FIND THE ANIMAL
A·B·C

Best Wishes
To
Rosemary Courtney
love
Demi

For Eliza Hitz
who drew this horse

How to Play

Look closely at the drawing of the small unicorn in the box
on the facing page. Then find that little unicorn somewhere in
the drawing of the big unicorn. Play this Find-the-Animal game
on every page. Answers to the picture puzzles are given at the
end of the book.

DEMI'S
FIND THE ANIMAL
A·B·C

an alphabet-game book

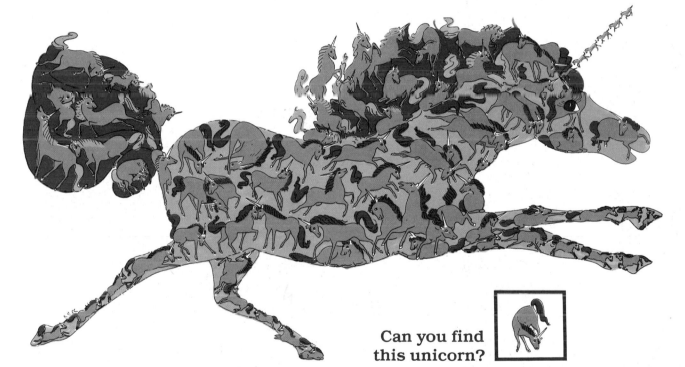

Can you find
this unicorn?

GROSSET & DUNLAP

Copyright © 1985 by Demi. All rights reserved. Published by
Grosset & Dunlap, a member of The Putnam Publishing Group,
New York. Printed in Italy. Library of Congress Catalog Card
Number: 85-70285   ISBN 0-448-18970-4   A B C D E F G H I J

Aa

Can you find
this alligator?

Bb

Can you find this bird?

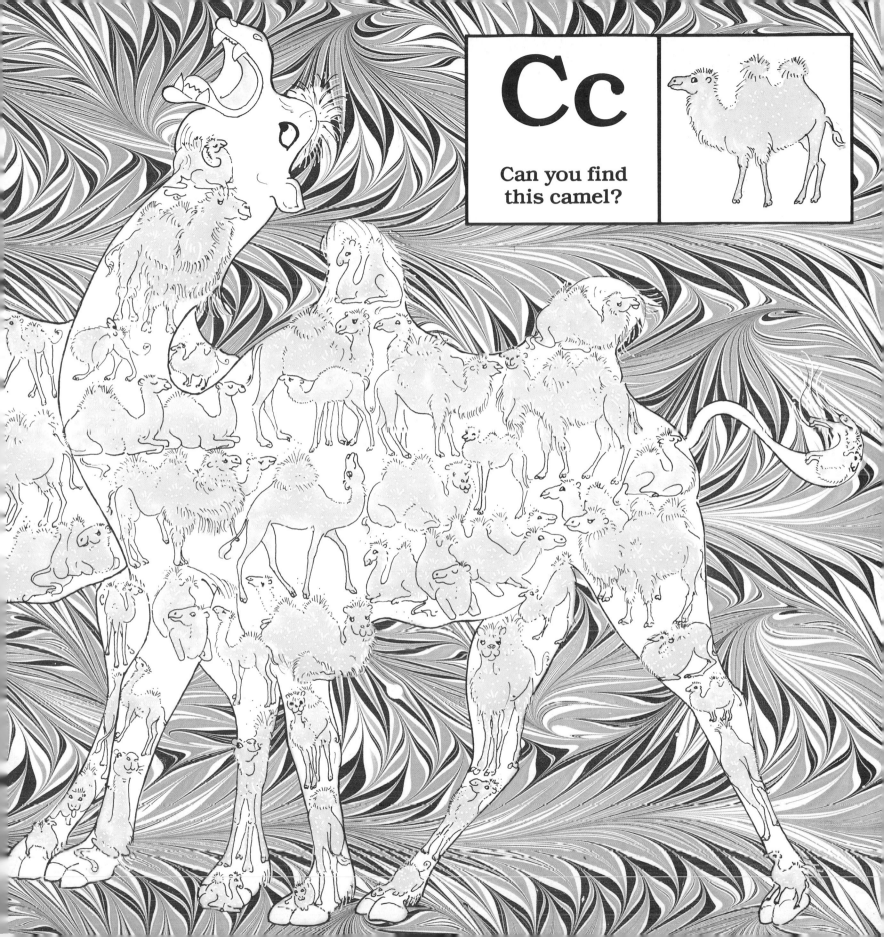

Cc

Can you find
this camel?

Dd

Can you find
this dog?

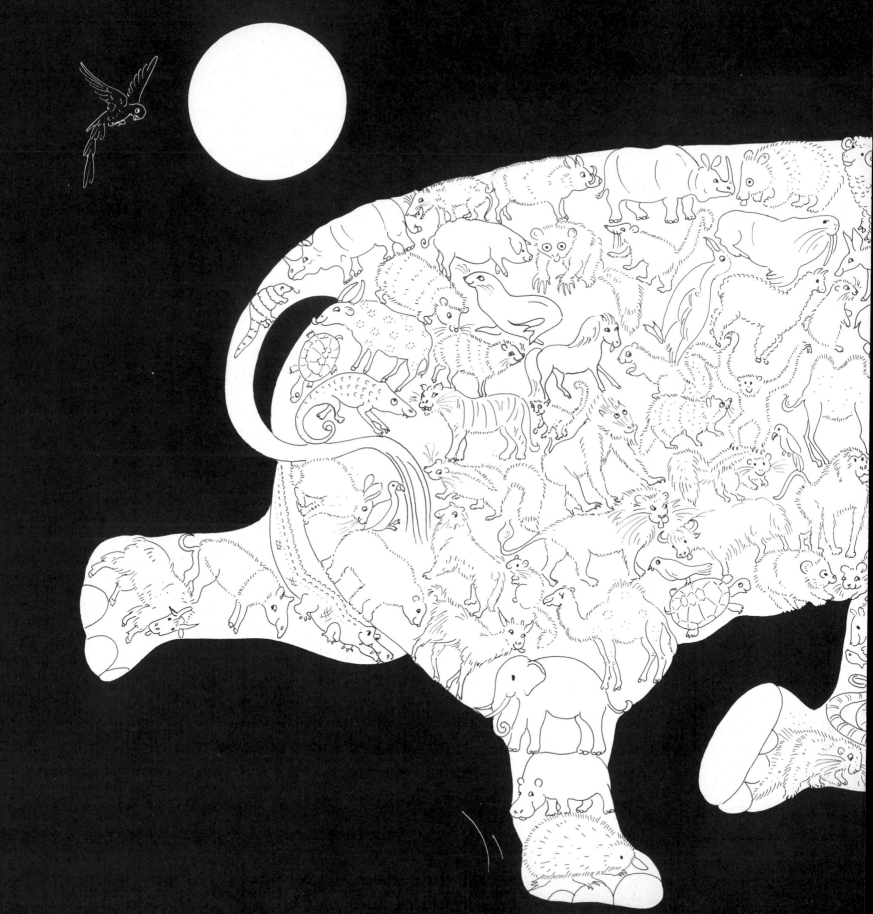

Ee

Can you find
this elephant?

Ff

Can you find
this fox?

Gg

Can you find
this giraffe?

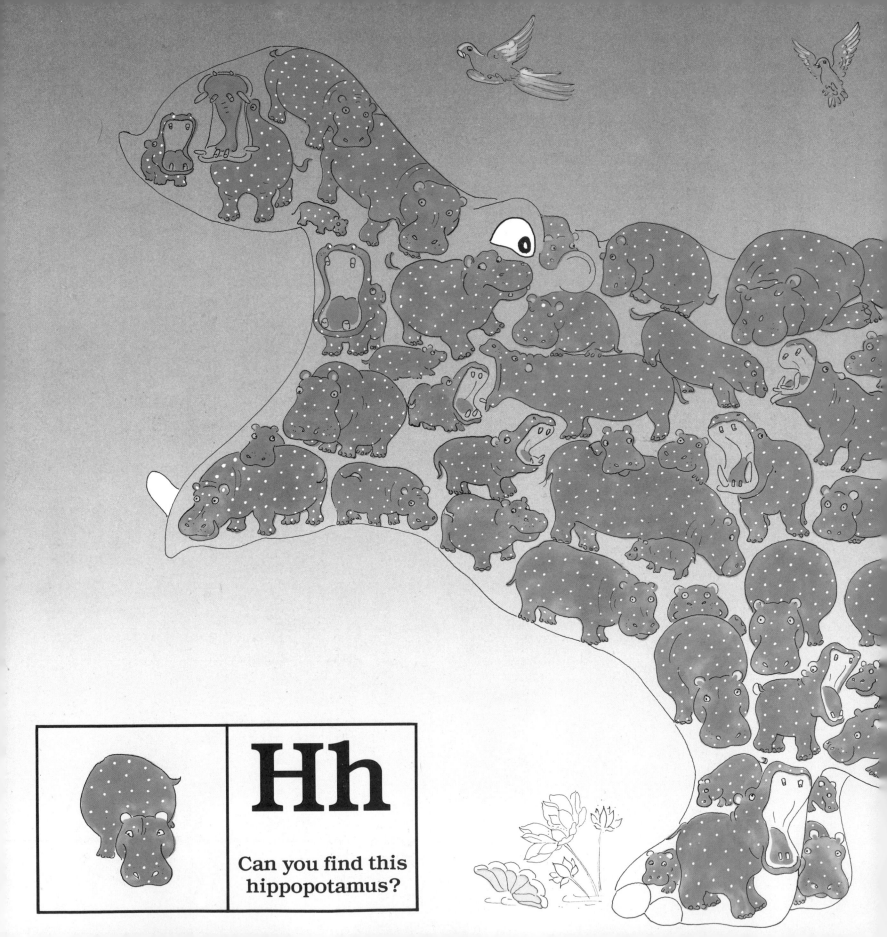

Hh

Can you find this hippopotamus?

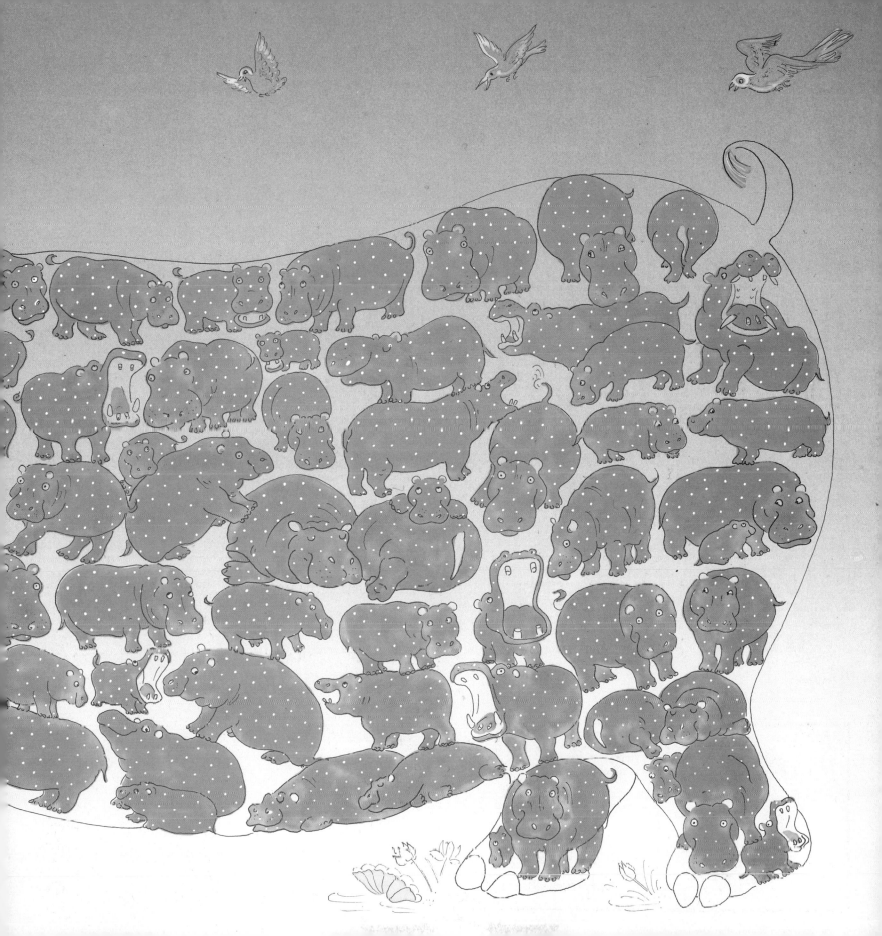

Ii

Can you find
this ibis?

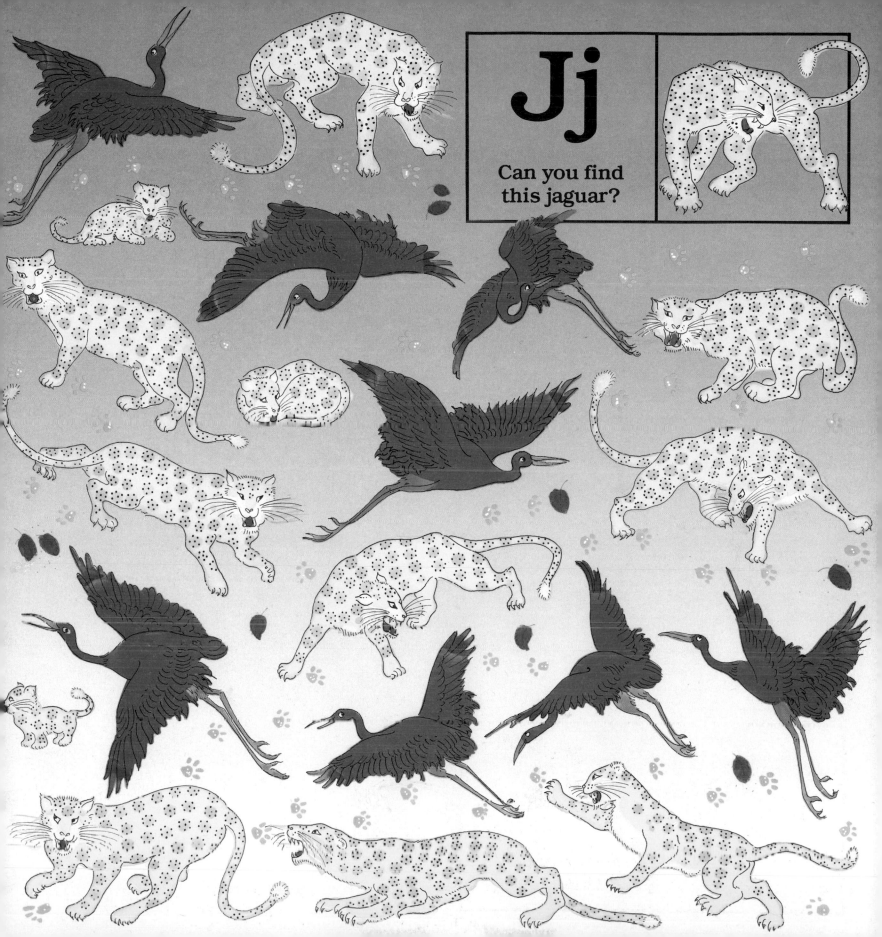

Jj

Can you find
this jaguar?

Kk

Can you find
this kangaroo?

Ll

Can you find
this lion?

Mm

Can you find
this monkey?

Nn

Can you find this nine-banded armadillo?

Oo

Can you find this ostrich?

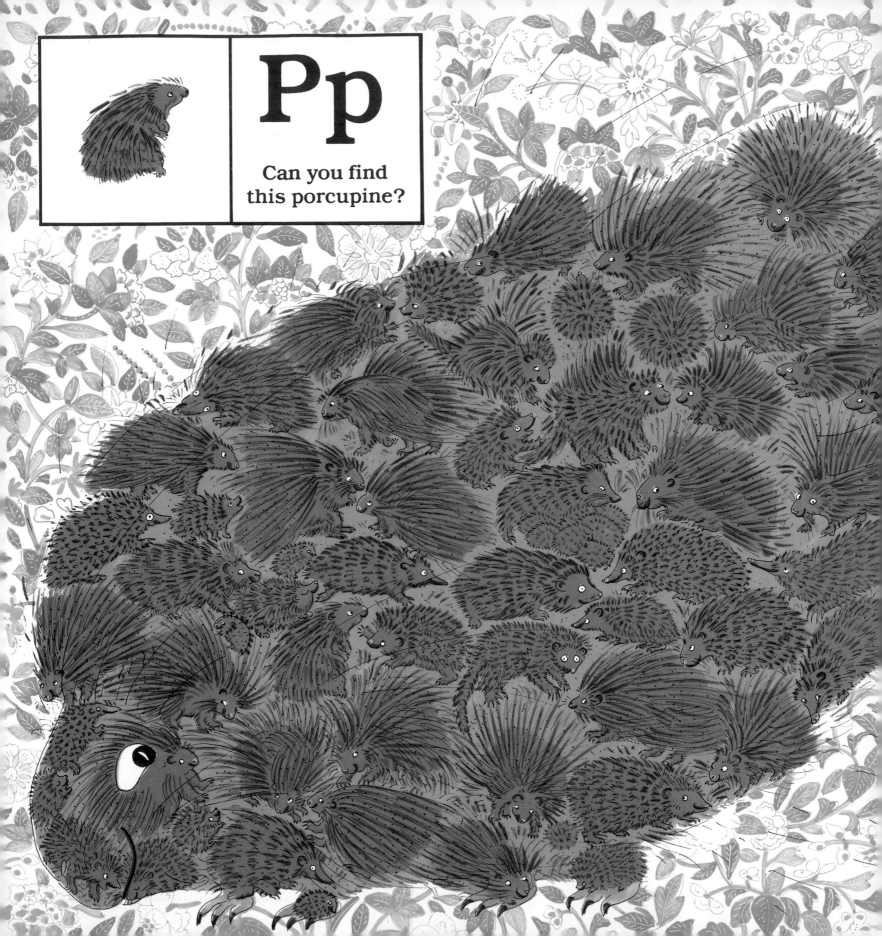

Pp

Can you find
this porcupine?

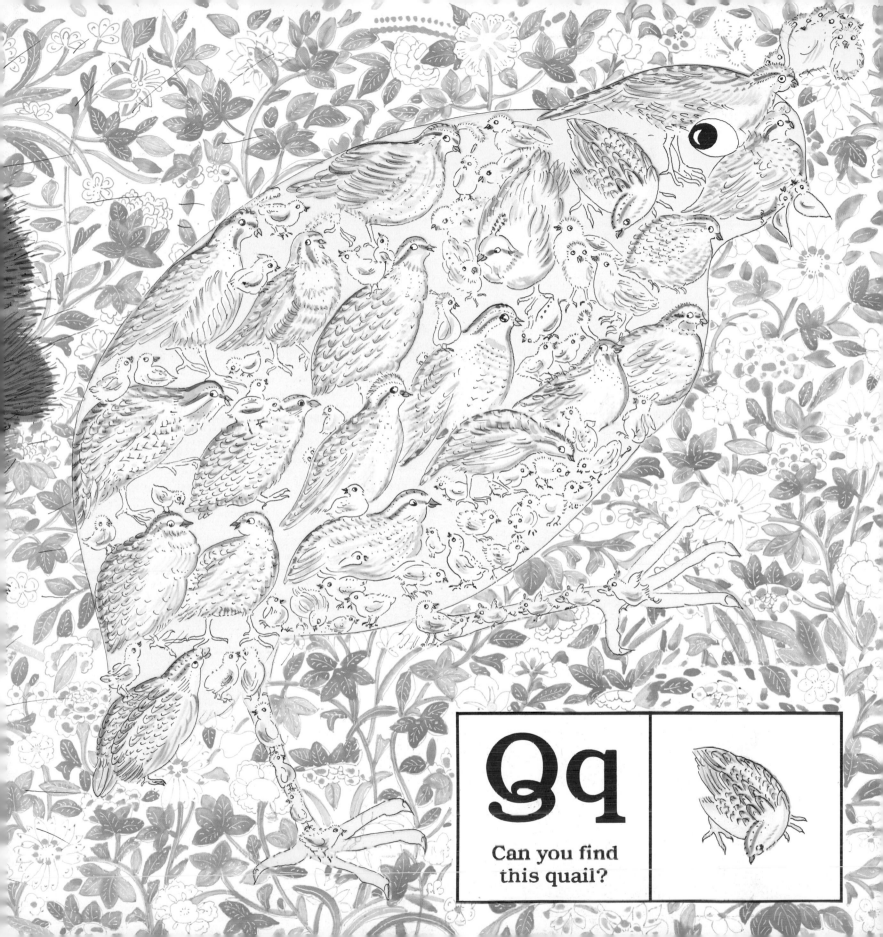

Qq

Can you find
this quail?

Rr

Can you find this rabbit?

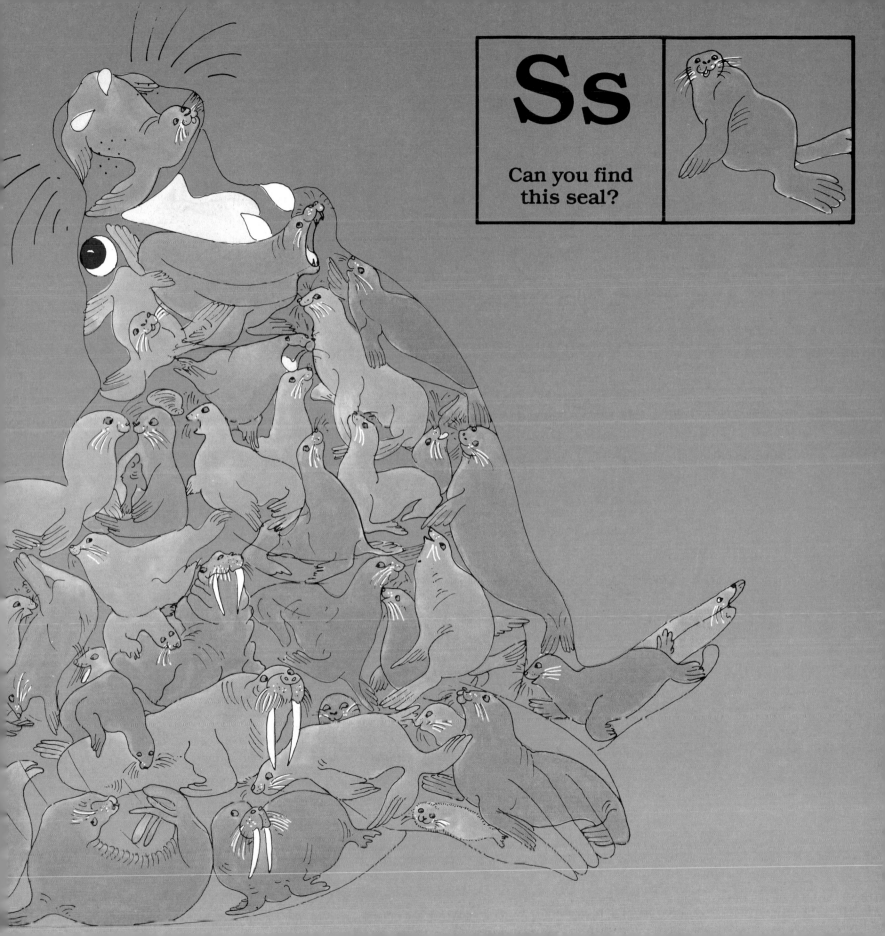

Ss

Can you find
this seal?

TURTLE RACE

Tt

Can you find
this turtle?

FINISH

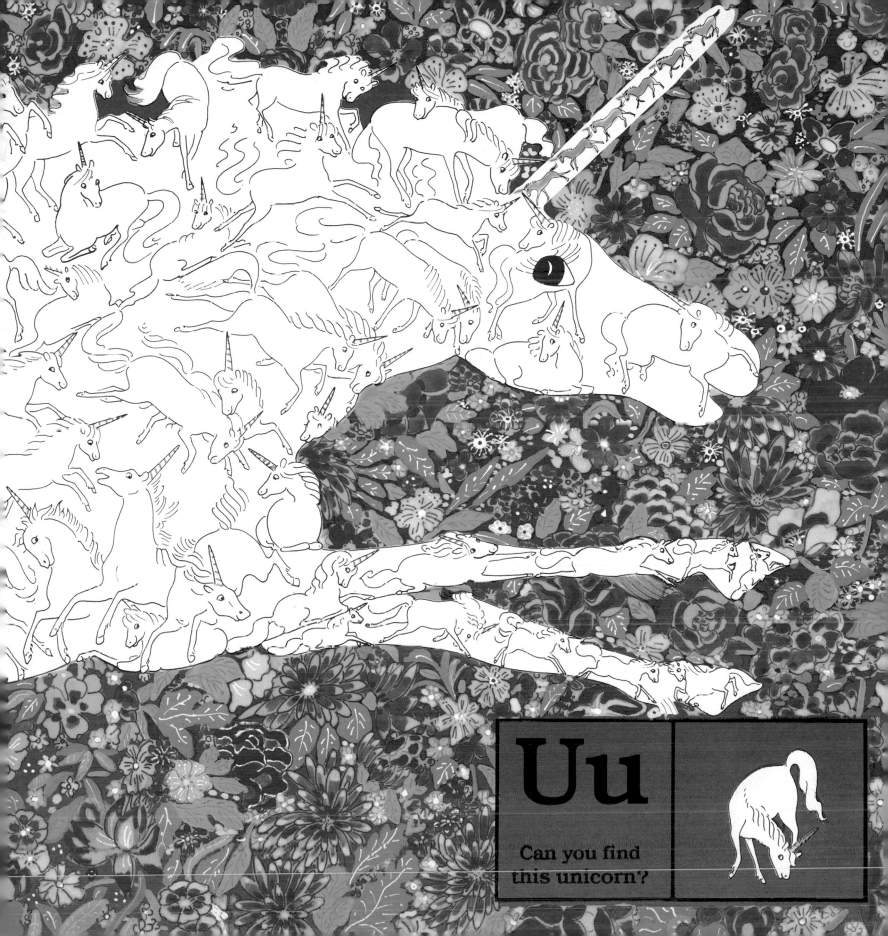

Uu

Can you find
this unicorn?

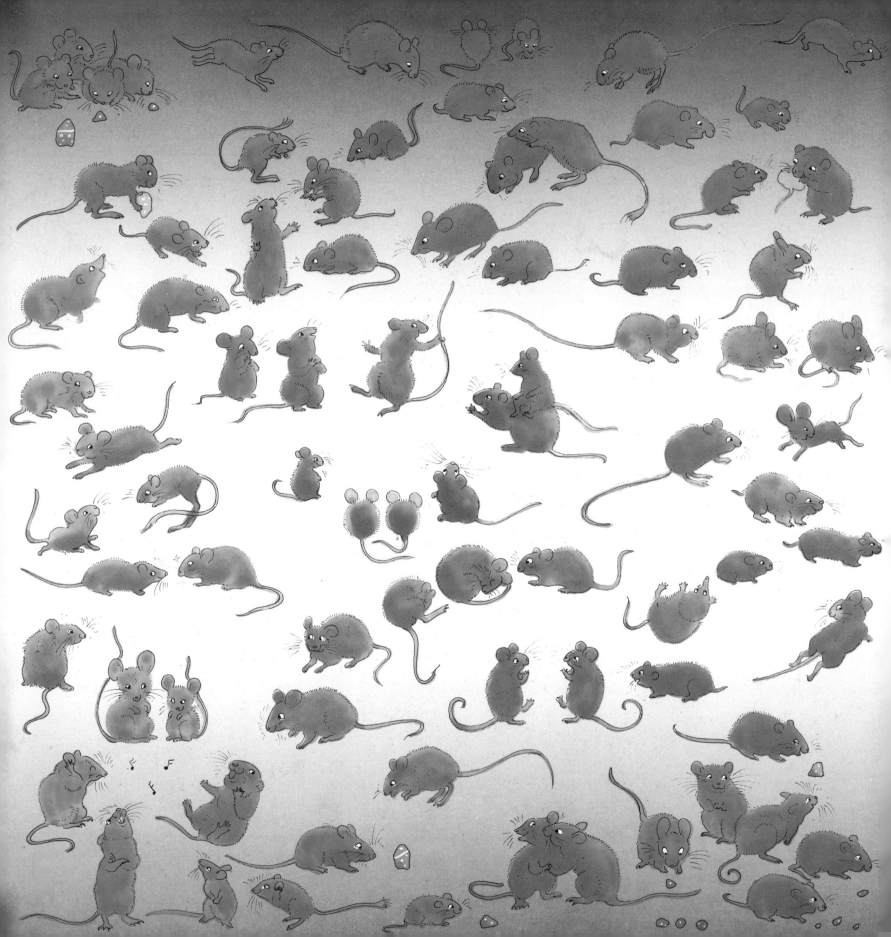

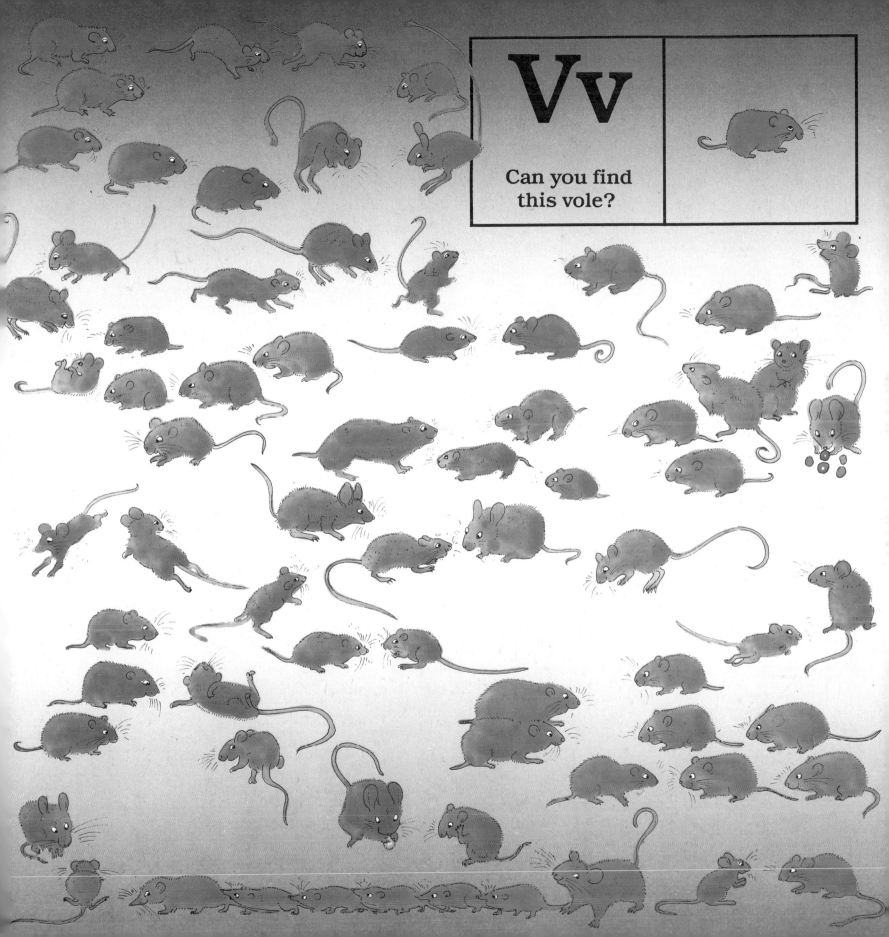

Vv

Can you find
this vole?

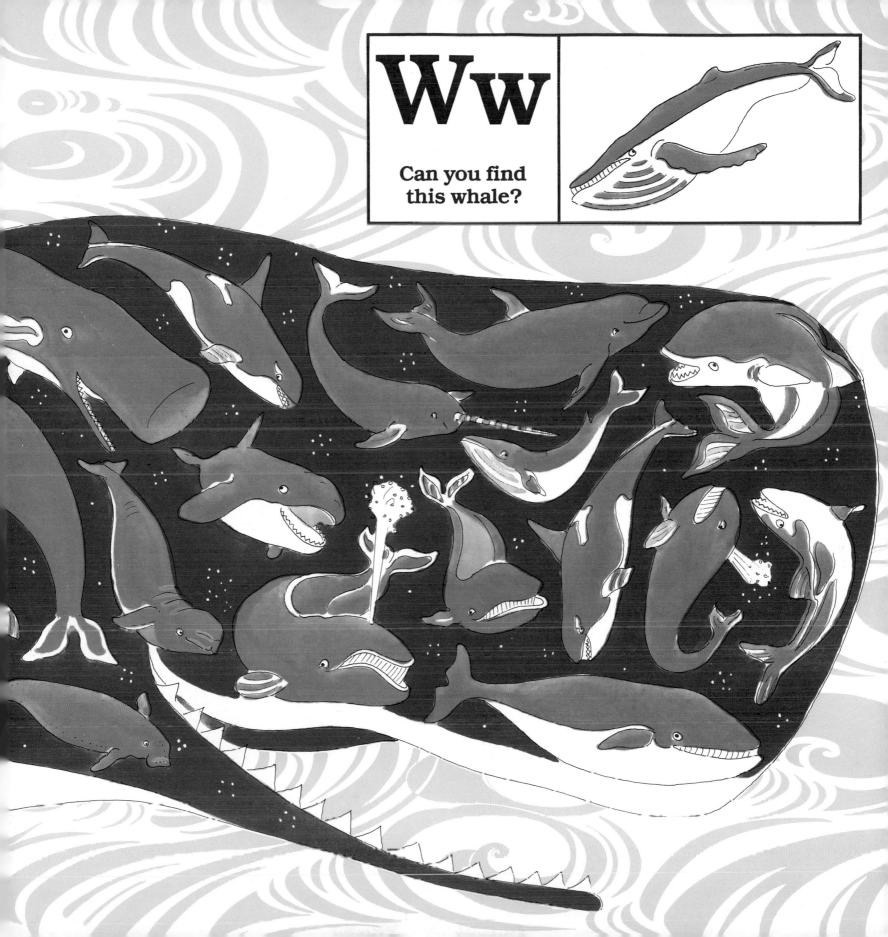

Ww

Can you find this whale?

Xx

Can you find
the X-ray fish?

Yy

Can you find
this yak?